O9-BTJ-191

This book is for Kitty Winn,
with Kitty knows what and Kitty knows what for
—J.S.

With love to Kristen and Alex
—J.M.

Text copyright © 2010 by Jon Surgal
Illustrations copyright © 2010 by Joe Mathieu

Published in the United States by Random House Children's Books,
a division of Random House, Inc., New York.

Beginner Books, Random House, and the Random House colophon are
registered trademarks of Random House, Inc.
The Cat in the Hat logo ® and © Dr. Seuss Enterprises, L.P. 1957, renewed 1986.

Visit us on the Web! www.randomhouse.com/kids

Educators and librarians, for a variety of teaching tools, visit us at www.randomhouse.com/teachers

Library of Congress Cataloging-in-Publication Data
Surgal, Jon.
Have You Seen My Dinosaur? / Jon Surgal ; illustrated by Joe Mathieu. — 1st ed.
p. cm. — (Beginner books)
Summary: A five-year-old boy searches high and low for his missing dinosaur, and the people
he asks for help do not believe such a creature actually exists.
ISBN 978-0-375-85639-6 (trade) — ISBN 978-0-375-95639-3 (lib. bdg.)
[1. Stories in rhyme. 2. Dinosaurs—Fiction. 3. Lost and found possessions—Fiction.]
I. Mathieu, Joseph, ill. II. Title.
PZ8.3.S966Hav 2010 [E]—dc22 2007043166

Printed in the United States of America
21

First Edition

Have You Seen My Dinosaur?

by Jon Surgal
illustrated by Joe Mathieu

BEGINNER BOOKS®

A Division of Random House, Inc.

Have you seen my dinosaur?

He's large. He's green. He likes to roar.

He sometimes likes a little drink.
So have you seen him in the sink?

Or could he be outside the door?

Please, have you seen my dinosaur?

I have not seen your dinosaur.

There's no such creature anymore.

I have not seen him in the sink.

He would not fit in there, I think.

I KNOW he's not outside the door!

I have not seen your dinosaur!

I've got to find my dinosaur.

He's never once been lost before.

He's hard to miss. He's very large.

He's larger than a river barge.

He likes to take a nap at four.

Please help me find my dinosaur.

I cannot find your dinosaur.

There's no such thing, not anymore.

A dinosaur cannot be found—

From deepest deep to highest ground.

From shore to ship or ship to shore,

You will not find your dinosaur!

I lost my dinosaur today.

Do you suppose he ran away?

Could he be hanging from a kite?

Or hiding somewhere in plain sight?

He likes to watch me comb my hair.
This morning, though, he wasn't there.

I thought that he was in the shower.
Oh, he can shower for an hour.

He might be in some big desk drawer.

Please, have you seen my dinosaur?

You say you've lost a dinosaur?
A strange thing to be looking for!
A thing as tall and wide as that
You won't find underneath a hat!
If I were you, I'd get a cat.
Or dog. Or bird. Or small white rat.

Have you seen my dinosaur?

It's teatime. It's his turn to pour.

A Scottish beastie from Culloden.

A big black bear from Baden-Baden.

Plus two gnu. A kinkajou.

Camels with one hump or two.

Now let me see. What have we got?
A lynx. Some minks. An ocelot.

A shaggy yak from far Bhutan.

An upside-down orangutan.

A fat wild boar from East Timor . . .

But no, we have no dinosaur.

There aren't any, anymore.

We do not have your dinosaur.

I need to see Professor Pew.

I'm Pew. What can I do for you?

I'm looking for a dinosaur.

What kind is it you're looking for?

His tail is longer than a mile.
His neck is longer still. His smile
Gets wider every time I see him.
  You need to try a big museum.

Is this the place where, people say,
A dinosaur is on display?
Sure is. Now let me think. (It's tough,
Because we've got a LOT OF STUFF.)

Look! Statues made by ancient Greeks!
To name them all would take me weeks.
But not a single statue here
Is of a dinosaur, I fear.

These paintings are all very rare.
No photos, please! Stay back, take care!

· MONA LISA ·

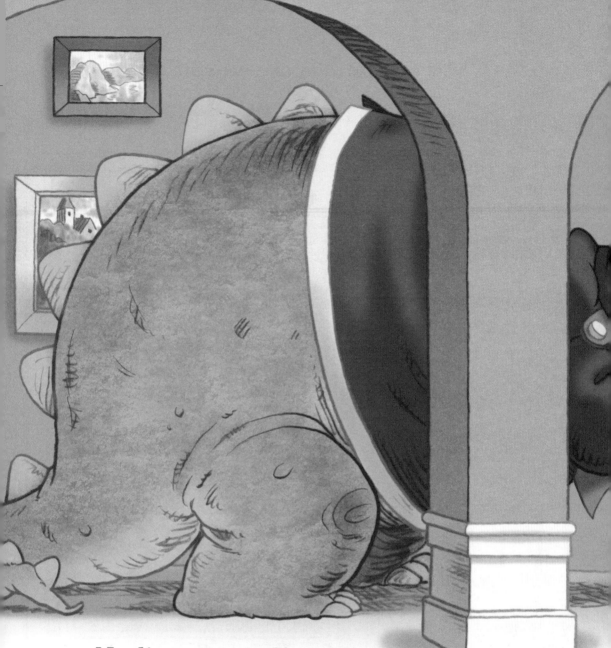

No dinosaurs in here, I'm told,
Although our paintings are quite old.
Of course, they're dusted now and then
By trusted, well-trained handymen.

Here! Here is what you're looking for!

Here's where we keep our dinosaur!

It lived a long, long time ago,

Two hundred million years or so!

Two hundred million years ago?

No! No! No! No! That can't be so!

This isn't what I came to see!

My dinosaur is five, like me!

A year ago, we both were four!

WHEREVER IS MY DINOSAUR?

I've got to find my dinosaur

Before he misses one meal more.

But where a dinosaur might go

Is something no one seems to know.

My mother did not have a clue.

The fisherman did not come through.

It stumped the whole police force too.

I got no further at the zoo,

Or when I saw Professor Pew.

The big museum had nothing new.

So what, oh what, am I to do?

I think who I should ask is . . . you!

Have YOU seen my dinosaur?

You have?

He's where?

Say that once more!

A dinosaur's a kid's best friend.

But hide-and-seek is hard!

The end.